Ex Libris

for Sophie — with love

Light Horse Boy is based on the historical events of 1914–1918. Jim, Charlie, Bob and Chook are fictitious characters created after researching the records and diaries of Australian and New Zealand soldiers who served in the 'Great War'. I have placed Jim and his mates in the 4th Light Horse Regiment but to maintain an interesting sense of story, and to enable me to recount aspects of less explored units such as the Medical Corps and LH Field Ambulance, I have taken some liberties with Jim's movements. To ensure Jim and Breaker remain together, I have also moved them more than would probably have occurred. I have endeavoured to portray details regarding specific campaigns and battles as accurately as possible from a firsthand, but sometimes limited, point of view.

The photographs accompanying this story are from World War One, but do not always reflect the exact battle or location described in the text.

After the War, many of the Walers serving in Europe were auctioned from the Calais Remount Veterinary Hospital. The horses in the Middle East were not so fortunate. Official instructions were to destroy older horses. Younger horses were to be sold. Many soldiers chose to shoot their beloved Walers rather than leave them behind to an unknown fate.

Of the 136,000 Walers that left Australia, only one returned. After being hit by a sniper's bullet at Gallipoli, Major General Bridges' dying wish was for his much-loved horse, Sandy, to be sent home. Sandy travelled from England on the freighter *Booral* and spent the rest of his life grazing peacefully in the Melbourne suburb of Maribyrnong. The only fallen Australian to be returned from World War One was Major General Bridges. After initial burial in Alexandria, the Major General's body was exhumed and his final resting place is on a hillside overlooking the Duntroon Military College in Canberra.

Dianne Wolfer

For more background information please visit www.diannewolfer.com
Teaching notes are available at www.fremantlepress.com.au

Light Horse Boy

Dianne Wolfer

illustrated by Brian Simmonds

FREMANTLE PRESS
fremantlepress.com.au

*J*im stared across the paddock as his best mate galloped towards him.

'Have you heard the news?' yelled Charlie. 'Britain has declared war on Germany. The army is recruiting. We could both join up. Wouldn't that be a lark?'

'But I'm not eighteen ...'

'When they see how you ride, they won't ask for a birth certificate.'

'You reckon?'

'Too right! The Light Horse would be mad not to take you. You're not scared, are you?'

'Course not!'

'Well then? This is our chance to see the world. The war will be over in a few months and we'll miss the fun if we wait.'

Jim rubbed his blistered hands. Fighting Germans would be a lot more exciting than digging post holes.

He frowned, wondering what his sister would say.

'We'll make crackerjack soldiers,' Charlie coaxed.

Jim laughed.

'Righteo,' he agreed. 'I'll be in it.'

They rode into Mansfield. The recruitment tent was pitched on the showgrounds. Charlie showed off with some fancy riding and the officer gave him a nod. Then the sergeant turned to Jim.

'Are you sure you're old enough to sign up?'

'Yes, sir.'

'I can vouch for him,' Charlie said.

Jim tapped his heels against Breaker's belly and pressed his knees into the gelding's ribs. 'C'mon,' he muttered. 'Let's show them what we can do.'

They cantered towards a high fence. Breaker cleared it easily.

'Well done,' Jim whispered, rubbing Breaker's neck. He was bursting with pride to be riding a stockhorse with such spirit.

'You're a fine horseman, son,' the sergeant said.

'And I'm a farrier by trade, Sir.'

The older man smiled. 'We need farriers. If the doc says you're fit, I'll be glad to take you.'

8 August 1914

Dear Alice

Soon I'll be sending news that isn't about rabbits, dust and damper. Charlie and I want to do our bit for the Empire so we've joined the Light Horse. Don't be cross that I fibbed about my age. It's only seven months until I really am 18 and I'm desperate not to miss out. The Boss was sad to see us go, but said that if he was young enough, he'd enlist too. He gave me his best horse in place of my wages and Alice, Breaker's a beauty.

My hands were shaking as the doctor checked my teeth and peered into my ears, but guess what? I passed with flying colours. Your little brother is now a fair dinkum Light Horse man of the Australian Imperial Army. Charlie passed too, so we'll be riding off to war together. It will be such an adventure.

The veterinarian gave us £30 for supplying our own horses and in the morning we'll travel to the Broadmeadows Training Camp. I can't wait! Charlie sends his best wishes and says to tell you he promises to look out for me.

You can send mail to the address on the envelope and the army will forward it.

Love from your soldier brother,
Jim

PS I hope the twins are behaving.

Alice McDonnell

The Governess

Glengarry Homestead

Fern Tree Gully

Victoria

After reporting to the quartermaster, Jim tied Breaker onto the horse line and unrolled his swag.

'What a day,' he sighed, gazing up at the Southern Cross. Then he rolled over and slept like there was no tomorrow.

In the morning Jim and Charlie joined the other recruits to march and ride along Mansfield's main street. As the townsfolk waved Union Jacks, Jim grinned and tried to make Breaker march in time.

Dear Alice

Thanks for your letter. Being a soldier is terrific
and I promise to be careful. All is tip-top here. We're
camped in a paddock ten miles from Melbourne.
Breaker has settled in well. It's been hard slog
with drills and what not and it's freezing, but our
uniforms are made of good, thick wool.

   Here's what the quartermaster gave us:
   - An AIF jacket
   - Cord riding breeches and leggings
   - A slouch hat, and best of all ...
   - A bandolier that holds 90 rounds of ammunition.
   We can't stop admiring
ourselves. Charlie reckons the girls
will be swooning when we ride into
town.
   I wish Mum and Dad could see
me in my new kit. Some nights I
imagine them looking down from
above.

Jim

Dear Jim

I'm not happy about your decision, but I'm proud that you're doing what you think is right.

How marvellous that your dream of owning a horse has suddenly come true. The twins were very excited to hear about Breaker, but Fred was even more ____ l by the thought of your bandolier and rifle. He and Bessi___ ___ day now. Fred has suggested that th___ ___ is quite a thrill f___

16 August 1914

Hello Sis

There are over 2,500 soldiers now: field artillerymen and infantry as well as our Light Horse Regiment. This morning we dug latrines and pitched tents. There are eight men in each tent and we sleep with our legs stretched into the centre like spokes in a wheel.

Our horses are tethered outside. There are some handsome animals, but none as good as Breaker. I still can't believe he's mine.

We're divided into four-man teams for training. Charlie and I joined two blokes from Gippsland. Chook is a butcher by trade and Bob is an office clerk. The four of us share our tent with another team from different parts of Victoria. Two are shearers, one's a baker, and there's another farrier like me.

Speaking of bakers, I was as surprised as you to hear about old Mr Becker. I'd never thought of him as being a German. I wonder who'll run the bakery while he's under camp arrest?

*W*ith so many horses, there was plenty of work for a farrier. The lads in Jim's unit praised his horse skills. He shrugged it off, but secretly their words made him proud.

When he wasn't checking hooves, Jim admired his new equipment. Breaker's military saddle was built onto padded wooden bars and Jim strapped his greatcoat and ground sheet across the front of it. His mess tin, a billy, canvas water bucket and nosebag of grain were slung on the back. Jim also had to find room for Breaker's heel rope and spare horseshoes. Galloping with so much equipment was awkward, but Jim soon got used to it.

As he and Breaker trained, a deep bond developed between them. Soon they'd depend on each other for their lives.

Sunday 6 September 1914

Hello Sis

Our Light Horse equipment is first class, but it's a devil of a job to pack. You would have laughed the first time I tried to load Breaker. Bits and pieces were hanging everywhere!

Charlie says thanks for your cheerio. We hope to sail soon. Every day there's fresh talk of our departure. We call the rumours furphies because we hear them at the Furphy water cart. It's a beaut invention, Sis — a big tank mounted on wheels.

This morning all units assembled for church parade. When our choir sang 'Onward Christian Soldiers' the sound of so many voices gave me goose bumps. Remember how Mum loved that hymn?

I'm learning so many new skills, Alice. Even my shooting has improved.

I hope you'll be able to visit before we leave.

Did I tell you about our mascot? Most of the units have dogs, but Chook smuggled in a rooster! We've called him Billy and he loves perching in strange places.

20 September

Dear Jim

Seeing you was such a treat. You look dashing in your uniform and yes, Breaker is by far the most handsome horse in the regiment!

I came home to find that the lads on the neighbouring farm have signed up and so the whole district is buzzing with talk of the war. The Boss wants to enlist, but the Missus is dead against it. They had a terrible row last night.

What did you think about South Melbourne's win over Carlton? Looks like it will be an exciting Grand Final. I wonder whether you'll have sailed by then?

While Jim and Charlie trained at Broadmeadows, troops were gathering in ports across Australia. On the other side of the Tasman, New Zealand soldiers were also waiting to sail, but their departure had been delayed. The German warships, *Gneisenau* and *Scharnhorst*, were at large in the Pacific and one raider, the *Emden*, had captured more than a dozen ships in September. It was too risky for the New Zealanders to sail without an escort.

In early October the Japanese battleship *Ibuki* and HMS *Minotaur* were sent to accompany the Kiwis from Wellington. The convoy could begin at last.

Broadmeadows Training Camp hummed with last-minute preparations. Hammers rang on anvils throughout the day as Jim and other farriers reshod the horses. After Jim clipped the last hoof of the day, he packed two kitbags — one for taking on board and another to store in the ship's hold. Then he rushed out to send a telegram to Alice.

E.T. No. 3. COMMONWEALTH OF AUSTRALIA.

Postmaster-General's Department, Victoria.

No. 45

OFFICE DATE STAMP

URGENT TELEGRAM.

This message has been received subject to the Post and Telegraph Act and Regulations.
All complaints to be addressed in writing to the Deputy Postmaster-General.

REMARKS

STATION FROM, No. OF WORDS, AND CHECK.

NOTE.—The figures at the bottom represent the time lodged at Sending Station and time received at this Office respectively.

DEPART TOMORROW STOP LOVE
TO ALL STOP JIM

19 October 1914

Dear Alice

We're off to the war at last!

As our ship pulled away, Charlie, Chook and I tossed streamers to the prettiest girls. Bob's wife was on the wharf with his children. We could see the oldest lad comforting his mother. Once we cleared Port Phillip Bay the sea was rough. Breaker was sick all night, but this morning he's finding his sea legs.

I love walking along the lines chatting to the horses. We've laid strips of matting along the decks so we can exercise them. They hate being cooped up below. I'm getting to know the different horses. Some are nervy but they've never been to sea before so I don't blame them! Breaker is a champion. His temperament is all patience and gentleness. I'm afraid he'll lose condition on such a long voyage. One walk a day isn't enough.

I've been wondering about the fighting. I'm not afraid, I just hope that when the time comes, I'll be able to do my duty.

23 October

There's a huge swell today.

The horses are falling over in their stalls and one mare has died of pneumonia. We were told to expect losses, but we won't lose any more if I can help it.

We should be in Albany tomorrow, ready to rendezvous with the rest of the convoy. Still no sign of the German raider, Emden.

Dear Alice

Who would have thought I'd travel to Western Australia! Everyone is full of praise for the beauties of King George's Sound. We're anchored in a splendid harbour protected by two islands. Our convoy is a grand sight, Sis, and the Wiltshire is right up front beside our flagship, Orvieto. I'm so proud to be part of this.

Some troops have gone ashore to march but we're stuck on board. Bob and Chook are trying their luck with homemade fishing lines. They've already caught two whiting.

There's a lighthouse on one of the islands and Charlie is signalling to the lighthouse keeper's daughter. She's a whiz at semaphore, much faster than us. Her name is Fay. Charlie has asked her to send messages home, so don't be concerned if a telegram arrives.

I'm not sure when this letter will reach you. Mail will be held back until we're well out to sea. No one wants messages to fall into the wrong hands.

King George Sound in Albany
All our ships, ready to sail
October 1914.

Michaelmas Island   Breaksea Island

Miltiades
Omrah
Hororata
Star of Victoria
Rangatira
Benalla
Afric
Shropshire
Argyllshire
Euripides
Orvieto
Southern
Pera
Armadale
Saldanha
Katuna
Hymettus
Suffolk
Anglo-Egyptian

Waimana
Ruapehu
Orari
Athenic
Arawa
Tahiti
Limerick
Star of India
Hawkes Bay
Maunganui
Clan Maccorquodale
Morere
Karroo
Port Lincoln
Geelong
Star of England
Wiltshire ← me

One last note before we sail. I have some exciting news. The Orvieto needed a farrier and our veterinarian suggested me!

I was proud to be chosen, but didn't want to leave Breaker and my mates. I was also a touch nervous at the idea of being on Major General Bridges' ship, but the suggestion turned into an order and so here I am, hobnobbing with the officers and their horses on our flagship. Charlie has promised to look after Breaker until we get to England. I'll send more news from Ceylon.

Jim

*K*ing George Sound was calm as a millpond as *Orvieto* led the first column out to sea. She was followed by twenty-five Australian troopships with ten New Zealand vessels bringing up the rear.

As they passed Breaksea Island, Jim saw the lighthouse keeper's daughter waving with all her might. Jim grinned and waved back.

Orvieto waited behind Breaksea until all the ships fell into line. With 30,000 men and over 7,000 horses, the 1st Australian Imperial Force was the largest convoy the modern world had ever seen.

'What a fleet,' Jim whispered, feeling his chest swell with pride.

Once the sailing formation was complete, stokers heaved on coal and smoke plumes filled the air as the troopships steamed westward.

Two days later, on high seas in the midst of squalling rain, three dark shapes emerged from the mist: *Ascanius*, *Medic* and their Japanese escort, *Ibuki*. The troops gave a rousing welcome to the West Australians, who had sailed from Fremantle. Then the fleet set course for the Cocos Islands.

Monday 2 November 1914

Dear Alice

Orvieto is a grander ship than Wiltshire, with officers, clergymen and even nurses on board. What a sight it was as the fleet began smoking up. The billowing columns from our funnels were like inky fingers stretching to the heavens.

Here's something to make you smile — one soldier smuggled a joey on board and now it's hopping all over the ship. I've been asked to care for him and so far the little fellow seems healthy. We've called him Rufus and if you say the name aloud, you can guess why! I've made a collar from some old leather. Every morning I walk (hop!) him around the decks. You can imagine the comments.

There are twenty horses on board Orvieto and they're fine animals. I miss Breaker, but I've found a friend in the General's horse. He's a 16-hand chestnut called Sandy. I talk to him when I'm feeling homesick and he doesn't seem to mind.

This morning I was chatting away as I brushed Sandy and so didn't hear footsteps. When I turned I saw an officer standing behind me. My mouth dropped open when I realised it was Major General Bridges! I saluted — with the horse brush — and he laughed. Then he

asked about Rufus. We talked for a while before he continued on his way. I stood staring after him until Sandy nudged me to continue brushing.

The General seemed so ordinary.

Wednesday

We're in busy shipping routes now, so the lights are dimmed for security. The weather is terribly humid. It saps our energy and we get around in dungarees and singlets. The poor horses are struggling. Today we had jabs against typhoid and I'm feeling miserable. Sandy is off his tucker and I'm worried about him.

News just in via wireless: England has declared war on Turkey. I hope we'll be able to travel through the Suez safely.

Saturday

Dreadful squalls — the horses are having trouble standing. I hope Charlie is able to manage Breaker.

The Orvieto's veterinarian and I have worked around the clock tending cuts and bruises. Sandy is still off-colour and there's a new case of colic. This humidity is taking a toll on all the animals — except Rufus, who doesn't mind it at all.

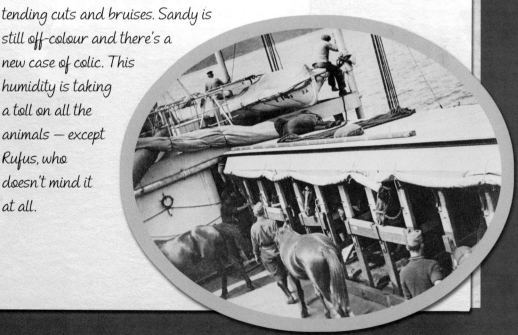

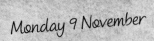

Monday 9 November

Great news, Alice

HMAS Sydney has sunk the Emden! This morning we received an SOS from the Cocos Islands and at 7am Sydney sped away. Suddenly the war felt very close. Ibuki raised her battle flag and moved beside Melbourne to protect the fleet. As we heard the boom of guns, I'm glad to say I was more excited than frightened. At last a message came through: 'Emden beached and done for'. We all cheered. Our first victory, Sis. Let's hope there'll be many more!

10 November

Three new cases of pneumonia and one is Sandy. General Bridges has been below deck most of the day. He has a gentle way with the horses and chats away to them like I do. Perhaps his aloofness with the troops is simply a mask for a shy nature. Hopefully I can't be court-martialled for thinking such things!

The weather is unbearable — it's like we're sailing into an enormous camp oven. Another horse died last night, but Sandy is holding on. My arms ache from massaging him. We've done everything we can. Now it's up to him.

12 November

Today we crossed the line. One officer dressed up as King Neptune, and there were games to celebrate, but with Sandy hovering on the edge, I couldn't enjoy it.

14 November

We're well past the Equator. The northern hemisphere doesn't feel different to our southern one, but by jove it's sultry. I have no energy. It's as if I've been drugged. One good thing is that we sleep on deck now. It's bonza sleeping under the stars in mid ocean. I watch them twinkle and remember your stories about the constellations.

15 November

Sandy has pulled through. The General was appreciative of my efforts. 'Going above and beyond,' he called it. I'm just happy he's well again.

We saw large shoals of flying fish today. They're very pretty and they can fly 100 yards! Soon we'll reach Colombo and I'll be able to post these letters.

Later

HMAS Sydney came into harbour with her decks crammed with wounded Germans from the Emden. We stood in silence, shoulder to shoulder, hats in hands, as she passed.

The smell was shocking.

The troops couldn't wait to receive mail at Colombo. After Jim settled the horses, he leant against a funnel and opened a letter from Alice. It was terrific hearing news from home and hard to believe it was only a month since they'd left. Jim laughed aloud at stories of the twins' latest mischief. Young Fred and Bessie certainly kept their governess busy.

Suddenly Jim heard shouts. A military guard was escorting German prisoners up the gangway.

Dear Alice

Your news from home lifted my spirits – it was as if you were here talking to me.

We've received prisoners from the Emden, some with terrible wounds. The Emden's captain is an imposing fellow and their torpedo officer is Prince von Hohenzollern, so now I'm sailing with royalty!

I was glad to hear that your friend Mary has become a nurse. The nurses on Orvieto are plucky girls, but I must say, when they're laughing together they make a chap nervous!

Monday 23 November

This morning we passed the island of Socotra. Its high mountains look barren and they say it's inhabited with cannibals. The sea here is full of jellyfish. They're a beautiful pink colour, like those ribbons on your favourite dress.

Our Major General Bridges is an early riser and he visits the horses every morning. Today as I organised the first feed, we were chatting about the high country and a canoe trip he took along the Snowy River. Who would have imagined that I'd have things in common with a Major General?

Alice, there aren't many opportunities to write uncensored mail, so I'm taking this chance to tell you something that might sound unpatriotic. Von Muller, the captain of the Emden, keeps to himself, but some mornings, when I exercise Rufus, he stands nearby watching us. And he looks so sad. He lost 134 men at Cocos. After beaching his ship, scores of men drowned or were impaled on the reef. Others died a dreadful death on the beach as seagulls pecked their open wounds.

The captain whispers to the horses in German and has what Charlie calls 'a knack with the nags'. I guess horses understand kindness in any language. Anyway, I have to keep reminding myself that he's our enemy. The Captain seems just like you and me, and poor Mr Becker. I hope I'll feel differently on the battlefield, but I needed to share this strange feeling with someone. Talking to you always helped me sort out my thoughts, and now writing has become my way of trying to make sense of things.

25 November

Our first sight of the African coast. They say 200 horses have died since we left Albany and I'm desperate to know how Breaker is faring. Maybe I'll see Charlie and the lads on Wiltshire when we arrive at Suez.

28 November

Still in the Red Sea. A wireless came through that we're being diverted to Egypt. No one is happy with the news. We signed up to fight Germans, not Turks.

Changing ships at Suez. There are miles of desert on both sides of the Canal with Indian troop defences. The calls of Egyptian hawkers spooked Sandy as we disembarked, so I've made a blindfold for him. No sign of Charlie or Breaker, but guess what I did see? A camel! They are the strangest creatures.

Later

We arrived in Alexandria with orders to remain on board, but after so many weeks at sea, we couldn't wait to see the sights. The officers turned a blind eye as we broke ship to enjoy a night in town. And Sis, the things we saw! The men here wear robes like long nightgowns with towel-like arrangements wrapped around their heads. They look as if they've just stepped out of the Bible.

10 December

Dear Alice

We're unloading the horses and I must say they're taking it well. Each one is lifted into a sling then hoisted over the side. They seem happy to be back on solid ground.

 Sandy is almost back to his old self again. The General offered me a position in his section, but I said I wanted to fight alongside my mates. I've been scanning the dock for them.

The troops reached Cairo in the evening, then began a ten-mile march to their campsite. Jim led Rufus along a path beside the River Nile, imagining pharaohs drifting along the dark waters.

At last they reached Mena. Jim wrapped himself in a thin blanket and slept where he fell. He woke to the amazing sight of pyramids glowing in the dawn light.

After helping pitch tents Jim went in search of his mates.

'G'day,' he hollered.

'Hello, stranger!'

Charlie roared with laughter when he saw Rufus.

'Trust you to find a roo.'

'Is Breaker alright?' Jim asked, looking around.

'He's fine. The horses are coming by train.'

'And Billy?'

'Still crowing at all hours.'

Jim helped his mates hammer tent pegs into the sand.

'It's good to have you back,' Chook said. 'The *Wiltshire* wasn't the same without you.'

Dear Alice

It's bonza being back with my mates. We've set up camp near the pyramids, surrounded by sand, which gets into everything.

Egypt is so different to home. You'd like the strange colours of the desert. The pyramids are the tombs of dead kings. The one we're camped next to belonged to a bloke called Cheops who lived around 2,500 BC. You can tell the twins that it's 470 feet high and made from over two million stone blocks. Imagine that! Bob says Napoleon camped here in 1798. He knows everything about this place.

Every day our camp gets bigger. There are thousands of men and all sorts of mascots. Lots of dogs, and one fellow even has a pair of monkeys. It's quite a menagerie.

The Egyptians have never seen a kangaroo, so Rufus has caused a stir. Meanwhile, Billy struts proudly about. None of the dogs dare bark at him. There are no trees to perch on, so we've set up a pyramid of rifles. Watching Billy balance there, trying to look important, always makes me laugh.

Breaker is thin. It's taken a while for him to regain his strength, but I'll soon have him in tip-top condition.

24 December 1914

Thanks for your parcel. The fruit cake was delicious. Bob said it was almost as good as his wife's, so that's high praise. We're feeling homesick as Christmas draws closer and disappointed not to be going on to England. Everyone here is itching to fight the Hun, but with Turkey joining the scrap, we're wondering what the New Year will bring.

An aeroplane flew overhead today — what a splendid sight.

Happy New Year, Sis

Climbing the blocks was hard work — they're bigger than they look — but the view from the top was worth it. We felt like kings of the castle sitting there trying to guess where we'll be next year. Probably back home after sorting out the enemy. We added our names to the messages carved over the top of the pyramid. Charlie wrote:

> Charlie and Jim
> from Bonnie Doon, Australia
> 1 Jan 1915

Then we made a pact to carve our names again at the start of 1916.

As the sun came up I wondered where Captain von Muller was spending New Year. I still think of him and I'll never forget the smell of the prisoners' wounds. Gangrene is a shocking thing, Alice. They were enemy soldiers, but I felt sorry for them.

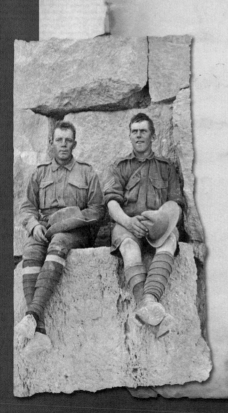

25 March 1915

Thanks for the good luck charm, Sis. It's a relief to not hide
my age anymore. We hired camels as a birthday lark and
Charlie led our unit to victory as we raced them.

There's talk that we'll see action soon, so I took Rufus to the
Cairo Zoo. He'll be safe there. We weren't the only unit with a
joey mascot. Rufus was hopping with excitement to meet other
kangaroos.

Something big is being planned. Our guess is that it's a
████████████ We've been practising ██████████████████
I can't wait.

*I*n May 1915, the Light Horse men left their horses in Egypt and sailed through the Dardanelles towards Anzac Cove.

As they passed Cape Helles, Jim and his mates cleaned the decks. Their transport would be returning with wounded soldiers.

The troopship steamed through the night. Jim heard the boom boom of big guns as they came to anchor. He peered at the craggy cliffs towering over a narrow beach, and couldn't imagine a worse landing place.

At last it was time.

'Here we go,' Chook muttered as they scrambled over the side. 'For death or glory!'

The ladder was slippery. Jim missed his footing and tumbled into the wooden transport.

'Steady,' Bob whispered.

Their captain gave the order to row. A few men joked and sang. Others prayed quietly. Jim wondered what Alice was doing at home as he tried to steady his breathing. Smoke puffed along the mountain top. As their boat rolled closer to shore, bullets suddenly splintered the water.

'Jump!'

Jim held his gun above the waves and kicked until he found his footing. There was little time to be afraid as he struggled through the water. Jim heard a cry. Bob lurched forward. Another volley of bullets screeched over their heads. Blood spread across the waves as Jim reached for Bob.

'Run!' Charlie called.

They were at the beach. Jim remembered Bob's family at the Melbourne wharf. He saw them waving. Rifle shots pinged the sand.

'Run!' Charlie yelled.

And Jim ran.

May 1915

Now I understand why the landing on April 25th is being called heroic.

We've landed in hell.

Bob didn't make it. He was hit as we struggled ashore. I keep going over that moment. Writing a letter to his wife was the hardest thing I've ever done. Harder even than going over the side of our ship.

We've taken a major hit. The casualties are shocking. There are long lines of wounded. Our unit has dug in near the field hospital. Charlie and I have been temporarily rostered onto stretcher duty. The first aid I learnt on the Orvieto is coming in handy. Repairing men is not that different to fixing horses. The surgeon wants to keep me on and Sis, I do feel useful here, but Charlie and I want to join the fight. More wounded arriving. I'll write again when I can.

Jim

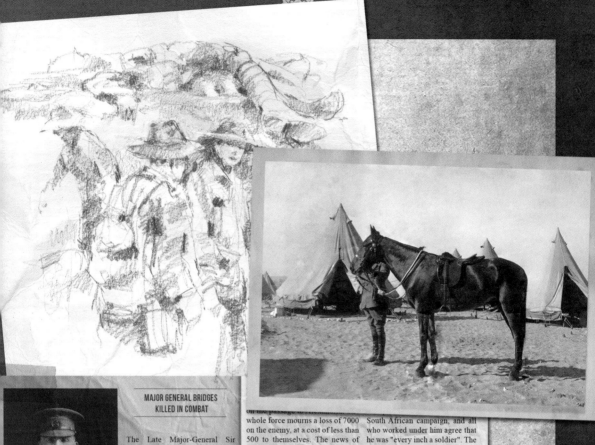

MAJOR GENERAL BRIDGES
KILLED IN COMBAT

The Late Major-General Sir William Throsby BRIDGES, K.C.B., Commander-In-Chief of the Australian Forces, who was wounded in the fighting at the Dardanelles and died at sea while being conveyed to the hospital at Alexandria, was buried at that city the funeral being quiet and impressive. General Maxwell commanding the British forces in Egypt, was present at the graveside. The following whole force mourns a loss of 7000 on the enemy, at a cost of less than 500 to themselves. The news of the distinguished officers death caused deep regret throughout Australia, for General Bridges was recognised as a brave leader and a brainy organiser and administrator. His work in connection with the Military College at Duntroon will serve as an imperishable monument to his zeal and energy. After vacating the position of Commandant of the Royal Military College, he South African campaign, and all who worked under him agree that he was "every inch a soldier". The posthumous honour of Knighthood (K.C.B.) was conferred by the King in recognition of General Bridges' distinguished services.

Such terrible news, Sis, we've just heard that Major General Bridges has died. He was hit by a sniper. Medics evacuated him to a hospital ship, but he'd lost too much blood.
I keep remembering his kind words to me during the voyage. They say the Major General's dying wish was for his horse Sandy to be sent home to Australia.

$\mathcal{T}$he hill had become a
rabbit warren of dugouts. Each day
Jim and Charlie scrambled along dark, tangled
gullies to collect wounded soldiers, but no matter
how hard they worked there were always more
waiting.

Bodies piled up between the trenches and on 24 May
an armistice was called. Troops from both sides lay down
their weapons to meet in no-man's-land. They separated the
heaps of decaying corpses and buried thousands of men in shallow
graves. When the armistice ended at 5pm, the soldiers went back to their
trenches, picked up their rifles and the bodies began piling up again.

$\mathcal{S}$corching temperatures in early June
turned the trenches into ovens. Hordes
of flies buzzed from dead bodies and open
latrines onto the soldiers. There was no water
for washing and it was impossible to keep flies away from hands, faces and
food. Conditions worsened as the summer heat intensified and disease
raced through the tunnels.

Dear Jim

It was kind of you to write and let me know about Bob's last moments. I had a strange premonition as your ship left and my greatest fear was that Bob would suffer. Knowing that he died quickly is a comfort.

Bob wanted to serve his country and we are proud, although it is hard to imagine life without him. Our oldest son does his best to be the man of the family, but he's only fourteen. He longs to sign up and I pray the War will be over before he is old enough. When you return I hope you will visit. May God keep you safe until then.

With grateful thanks,

Mrs Betsy O'Connell

July 1915

Dear Alice

This peninsula is a devilish place. The ground is covered in prickly shrubs and we're infested with lice.

Your Red Cross work is a great help and I think of you every time I unwrap a fresh bandage, wondering whether your hands prepared it. The lads are proud that our womenfolk are keeping the home fires burning. It will be strange coming back to a world where girls have taken all the jobs. They may not want to give them up!

We're working around the clock taking stretcher cases to the beach to be shipped back to Egypt. We use donkeys to help transport the wounded. They're plucky little beasts, but I miss Breaker's warm, oaty breath.

Charlie and I went down to the beach for a swim today. It was terrific to feel clean and we took great pleasure in drowning our lice. Enemy shells fall around us as we swim, but we duck dive before they hit the water.

10 July 1915

Bad news.

Chook took a hit in the arm and he's being shipped out. Charlie dragged him from no-man's-land and was able to stem the bleeding. Then we got him down to the beach and rewrapped his arm. It was shattered below the elbow and he'll probably lose it. Poor Chook, he was doing his best to keep in good spirits, singing 'Tipperary' so as not to cry out in pain. Now it's just me and Charlie from our original group.

War is not what we imagined, Alice. Instead of the grand excitement of a bayonet charge, we dig trenches and scurry through tunnels like rats.

August 1915 began with massive assaults on the Gallipoli Peninsula. After four months, the Australians were desperate to capture higher ground.

The infantry was in the thick of it, fighting for a strategic plateau which they called Lone Pine. The trenches were close. Two hundred yards from the firing line, Jim and Charlie watched a stretcher bearer return three times to bring in wounded soldiers. The third time he was shot through the head just before he reached safety.

There were more men to collect.

'Let's go,' Charlie whispered.

They rushed forward together and rolled a young lad onto their stretcher. Infantrymen dashed past them. The distance between trenches was barely a hundred yards, but dozens were mown down. Those that made it leapt into the Turkish trenches, struggling to drive back the enemy in dark, cramped tunnels. The fighting was savage — hand-to-hand — in an inferno of smoke and gunfire.

For five days and nights the hellish battle continued in the gloomy half-light of the bunkers. The Turks refused to surrender and the trenches were so narrow that to advance, someone had to be killed. Soldiers stood on their dying mates, fighting with bayonets, shovels, fists and picks. Wounded comrades were left untended and the piles of corpses grew to three and four men deep, in some places more. Black clouds of flies covered everything. It was impossible to talk or eat without swallowing them. Reinforcements spent their first hours vomiting uncontrollably at the stench of rotting flesh. Jim lost sight of Charlie on the third night. He continued on alone, helping the walking wounded until another shell gashed open his jaw and Jim's body at last collapsed.

$\mathcal{J}$im lay outside the trench, drifting in a strange in-between world where nothing mattered. Stars glittered in a cold sky while whispering shadows drifted around him. Dozens of men surrounded Jim but he'd never felt more alone. When at last the fighting ended, help came with a water flask and stretcher. Brackish fluid dribbled over Jim's chin and into his wounds. The pain stung him into consciousness and Jim knew it wasn't his time to die. Not yet.

Once his face was bandaged, Jim helped sort the bodies. Sometimes it wasn't possible to separate the Turks and Australians.

At last he found Charlie. And when he did, Jim wished he hadn't.

I have the worst news.

Charlie died at a place we've called Lone Pi...

They say it was once a shady grove. Now t...

trees are shredded. We weren't even meant

to be there but we'd been separated from our

mob and mucked in beside the infantry. It was

unspeakable Alice. I was hit in the face and have

lost a ...th, but I've been patched up and will

Dear Jim

I've been so worried. Please take care.

I want to do more for the war effort so I...
Purple Cross. We're helping raise money fo...
their country, and it makes me feel closer to y...
had a morning tea and I met Mrs Monas...
an inspiration.

So far we've raised enough to send twenty fl...
horses.

Love from all of us here, Alice

P.S Bessie and I are still knitting in the evenin...

October 1915

Dear Alice

Even on the high plains at home, I've never known such a bitter wind. It makes brave soldiers cry like babies. I'm out of the firing line for the moment, with my head bandaged up like Humpty Dumpty. I can only take liquid foods for a week, so no bully beef and biscuits. Apologies for the small print but paper has become rare as hen's teeth. Please thank Bessie for the socks. They fit perfectly, but Sis your letters warm me more than any woollen socks could.

Hello again

My face is healing so I've been allowed to rejoin my unit. In the morning, we'll go over the top. My luck can't hold on much longer and I don't expect to live.

   If this is my last letter, know that I'm not afraid to die. I'm proud to have done my duty and have made my peace with God.

   I hope Mum and Dad will be waiting, with Charlie and Bob, in a better place. You've been a wonderful sister, Alice. My thoughts are with you and my one regret is that my death will cause you pain.

Your loving brother, Jim

After months of fighting, the soldiers of both armies were exhausted. A stalemate arrived with the cooler winds and by November, storms lashed the battlefields. Somehow Jim had survived and as sleet cloaked the troops, his lips turned blue with cold.

The wind-whipped Aegean Sea became black and frothy. Torrential rain flooded the trenches and hundreds of soldiers drowned. They were too weak to escape. The rain also unearthed dozens of bodies from shallow graves.

Snowstorms followed the floods. Men froze to death and by early December the Anzac position was unsustainable. The officers made plans for evacuation.

20 December 1915

Dear Alice

We've left the peninsula at last and forty thousand Anzacs were evacuated without one casualty. Johnny Turk will be surprised to find us gone. We laid hessian sacks along the paths to muffle our boots. Then the last soldiers rigged up sand and water timers to fire triggers every five minutes. The officers say it's the best military hoax since the Greeks left their Trojan horse a few miles away at Troy.

We left the jetty, huddled on barges, keeping as quiet as possible, trying to swallow the bitterness of leaving our mates behind. I wasn't the only one who felt we were deserting them. We can't bring bodies home — there are too many — but leaving them in unmarked graves in these hills so far from home fills me with shame.

I keep wondering what Charlie and Bob sacrificed their lives for. I don't blame the enemy. They fought bravely to defend their homes. We'd do the same if they sailed into Port Melbourne.

26 December 1915

I spent Christmas at sea. We had fresh bread, pudding and extra serves of meat, bacon and cheese, but with so many mates left behind, it was a sombre meal this year. Now I'm back in

Egypt and as I stare at the pyramids, I can't believe Charlie isn't here.

Seeing Breaker was a treat. He's survived an outbreak of equine flu and is looking fit and well.

Dear Sis

This is a letter that I'll never post, but somehow writing it helps. Dying faces haunt my sleep. The smell of blood, vomit and fear. Dead mouths that scream forever.

How can I let go of the memory of burying Charlie? Of laying broken pieces of him into a common grave? Of scrambling to find his missing arm? The arm that cuffed me like a brother. Every night I search for that arm in my dreams. I never find it.

A handful of men, too old to fight on the frontline, had taken care of the horses while the troops served on Gallipoli. As Jim saddled Breaker, the jingle of riding spurs made him smile for the first time since Lone Pine.

Now that every waking moment wasn't spent trying to survive, there was more time to remember. The crisp Egyptian nights reminded Jim of autumn evenings back home. And Charlie. No matter how far he rode, Jim couldn't escape his memories.

When he wasn't on duty, Jim volunteered at the camp's veterinary hospital where one vet was responsible for more than two thousand animals. Hundreds of new recruits were arriving and as the camp grew, Jim helped check the horses' gums for colic and their hooves for seedy-toe.

1 January 1916

Dearest Alice

It's New Year's Day. I can't believe it was only last year that Charlie and I climbed Cheops' pyramid.

The new chums' excitement reminds me of our old group and our impatience to fight. Some Gallipoli veterans ask why these new recruits didn't sign up immediately. Where were they when we needed them? But Alice, our mob sailed off for an adventure. These new lads volunteered after seeing the casualty lists and I reckon that makes them even braver.

Another dust storm is building. The locals call them Khamseen and they're ferocious. The flying sand drives us mad. Sometimes it's so thick you can't see the man beside you.

Happy Birthday Jim

I have special news. Your friend Tom came to visit, and to let me know you were well when he last saw you. It was so very kind of him.

I hope you like this lavender sachet and that it reaches you before your special day. We've had lovely weather and the flowers are a treat.

Remember how Mum loved lavender? I thought you could keep this sachet close to your heart and the smell would remind you of home. It might deter the lice too!

28 February 1916

I'm glad Chook came to see you. It sounds funny when you call
him Tom. I forget he has another name. He's a terrific bloke,
Sis, and visiting you was probably more terrifying for him than
landing at Gallipoli.

    They're splitting the regiment soon and some lucky beggars
will be heading to ~~Europe~~. Not me unfortunately. Camp is
bustling. I keep looking for Sandy — Major General Bridges'
horse — but there are thousands of remounts, so it's like
searching for a needle in a haystack. No one knows whether the
General's wishes have been honoured.

$\mathcal{A}$s war raged across Europe, reinforcements were needed in France. In March 1916, ten divisions left Egypt whilst soldiers of the Light Horse remained behind to guard the Suez Canal.

12 April 1916

Dear Alice

Telegraphy will be a big change for Chook, but there'll be good prospects for him after all this is over.

We're still here in Egypt — still wiping dust from our ears, eyes and mouths. I'm sick to death of the sight of sand. It gets under the horses' shoes, too, so I'm always busy. Hundreds of Light Horse men have transferred to the infantry so they can fight in Europe. I'd love to get over to the real war, but don't want to leave Breaker.

We've been defending the Suez. It's a treat watching the great ships glide along and we are able to swim the horses. If the Canal is taken, England loses Egypt and access to her southern dominions, so we feel as if we're doing our bit. The sailors wave and cheer as their ships pass through.

5 May 1916

Hello Alice

We celebrated Anzac Day with a sports tournament. I was reluctant at first — Gallipoli is not a place I want to remember — but then I gave it my all and won two races for Charlie and Bob.

Between patrols our section has started a chess competition. We play during the heat of the day. It takes our minds off the insects.

The Turks launched an attack on our position. We've retaliated and are ready to ride at a moment's notice. Sometimes we march through the night. Lucky Breaker has a smooth gait and I'm able to sleep in the saddle. Our lads love outwitting the Turks then galloping away as their rifles spit puffs of sand around us.

German Taubes fly over almost every day now, but no casualties so far. As soon as we hear them, we jump onto our horses and gallop in all directions. Breaker thinks it's a game. The pilots have trouble seeing single horsemen in the desert, particularly if we stand still, so their shelling keeps missing us.

Taube means little pigeon in German, but Alice, these birds lay big eggs.

The soldiers of the Light Horse clashed with Turkish patrols as they fought along the Egyptian coast. When the horse lines came under aerial attack, Jim waved his fists at the enemy pilots.

'Come down here and fight!' he yelled.

The animals that weren't slaughtered broke their lines in a wild stampede and galloped into the desert. Jim rode after them grabbing the reins of riderless horses and bringing them back.

During one fierce battle, Jim stumbled upon a soldier lying in the shadow of his dead horse. Shrapnel had almost severed the lad's arm and he was barely conscious.

'What's your name?' Jim asked.

'Archie, but my mates call me Curly.'

The fellow's blonde curls were matted with blood.

Jim ripped his shirtsleeve into strips and made a tourniquet as gunshot pinged the sand around them.

'The Turks are over the next rise,' Jim whispered.

'Don't leave me.'

'No chance of that, digger.'

Breaker trembled as another bomb exploded,
but stood his ground as Jim draped the soldier over
the saddle. Jim swung up behind Curly and gave
Breaker his head. The old warhorse sniffed
the wind then carried them safely back to camp.

Watching men destroy each other is terrible, Alice, but targeting horses is somehow worse to me. German fighters swooped our horse lines and many brave animals have died. After the bombing I applied for a transfer to the Medical Corp. I'm sick of killing and want to help patch up some of the damage of war.

The field ambulance use the most reliable horses, so Breaker fits right in. He's teamed with three other Walers — that's what they call our Australian horses — pulling a dray and they're already great chums. In the field ambulance there are bearers, drivers and tent workers and we rotate jobs.

I seem to have a knack for settling both two-legged and four-legged patients and it feels like I've found my place.

Between raids Breaker and I ride to different units, checking the horses' hooves and mouths. Seedy-toe is rife at the moment and many Walers have septic sores. We also use camels to carry the injured — handling them isn't my favourite job — give me a horse any

July 1916

These endless skirmishes are keeping us busy.

I'm learning to drive a motorised ambulance. The speed is exciting, but there's no friendly whinny when you feed it.

August 1916

Dearest Jim

We see more and more cars here so knowing how to handle one will be a useful skill after the war.

Tom has been to visit — twice — and I hope you'll be pleased to hear that we're walking out together. The Missus sends the twins along as chaperones. Bessie thinks it's awfully romantic and I can't stop her questions. Young Fred idolises Tom, but I threatened to box his ears when he asked to see his wounds. I suppose it's natural for children to be curious, but poor Tom blushed.

Transporting the wounded is slow work and we're often between camps in the evenings. The desert is beautiful at night and sleeping under a sheet of stars in these Biblical lands is a magical thing, Alice. They're the same constellations I saw at Lone Pine, but they look different here. The brightest ones remind me of that ancient Star of Bethlehem.

This land has been home to countless battles and as I go on my rounds, I hear strange stories of soldiers seeing visions of horsemen and cameleers in old-fashioned uniforms. The warriors of the pharaohs, Persians and crusaders all fought here. As did the legions of Alexander the Great and Napoleon's army. This sand holds ancient skeletons.

I laughed at the ghost stories, until one of my mates saw a vision riding beside him. Another officer swears the air went suddenly cold when he heard the clink of an unfamiliar bridle. I've ridden through plenty of dust storms and have only seen sand, but who knows? That officer is normally a sensible fellow.

FOR CORRESPONDENCE | FOR ADDRESS ONLY

FIELD POST OFFICE
SEP 8 1916

Hello Alice, Now I know why desert creatures live underground. The weather is unbearable, with air so hot that it hurts when we breathe. Our water is rationed and what we have is murky stuff. We've come up with a clever ruse to protect the horses from German pilots. Our dummy horse lines are made from poles and blankets. Enemy aircraft target them while our Walers stay safe.

Alice McDonnell
The Governess
Glengarry Homestead
Fern Tree Gully
Victoria

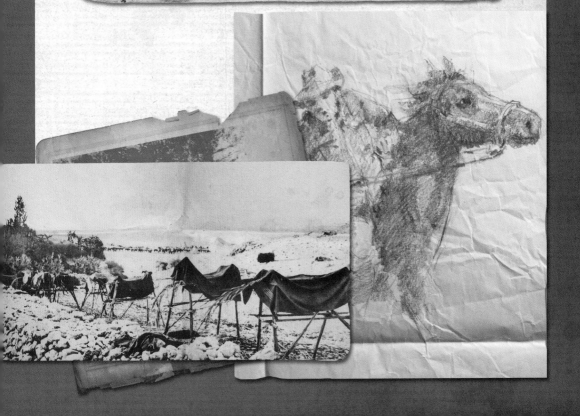

$\mathcal{I}$n December 1916, Harry Chauvel's Mounted Division and the Camel Corps continued the fight eastwards to El Arish then inland to the stronghold of Magdhaba.

As they marched through a chalky wadi, the horses' hooves kicked up a cloud of fine white dust and soon the horsemen were covered in powder.

'We look like phantoms,' Jim whispered.

Breaker snorted and the ghostly puffs above his nostrils made him even more wraithlike.

British, Australian and New Zealand troops fought through the day to win the town and by late afternoon Magdhaba was secured.

After thirty hours without water and an exciting final gallop, the horses were desperate to drink from the wells.

Following the battle, a roster for leave was drawn up. Jim's name was near the end and he spent another Christmas camped in the desert, wondering where to carve Charlie's initials on New Year's Day.

Dear Alice

Congratulations on your engagement. I was rather hoping that might happen. You couldn't have picked a better fellow to marry. Tell Chook he's a lucky man to have won my sister's heart! I'm so happy for you both. Good news for me, too, Sis, I've been promoted.

The troops ~~~~

Dear Jim

Another New Year without you. I pray it's the last.

I've been busy knitting socks for you. Tom said that's what you'd like. I hope you can find some way to celebrate and enjoy yourself, though I know it must be hard to even think about having fun after everything you have been through. I am so longing to get you home safely.

Tom and I have started making plans for our future together. Saying goodbye to everyone here — and especially the twins — is going to be difficult. I feel this is my second home. The Boss and the Missus have been so kind, and ~~~~~~~~~~ ~~ much pleasure (and sometimes anxiety!).

March 1917

Dear Alice

An unsuccessful attack on ~~~~~~~ The man beside me was blown to smithereens while I barely copped a scratch. We've withdrawn, I can't tell you where, but it's near a beach and swimming the horses is a welcome change.

A shipment of your Purple Cross packages arrived — just in time — the field ambulance horses all need new fly veils.

Dear Alice

Mail at last! Your wedding plans sound grand. I only wish that I was there to walk you down the aisle. Mum and Dad would be so proud of you, Sis.

I've had a few days leave in Alexandria and enjoyed my first bath since I don't know when.

This morning I visited Rufus at the zoo. He looks well, though I'm sure he'd like more space to hop. What a story he could tell those kangaroos back home!

Temperatures are soaring. The fleas are bad and the dust is terrible. Watering the horses is a constant challenge. That's where camels come in handy. They're funny things. Good for transporting soldiers and patients over long sandy stretches, but by jove they're temperamental and crikey do they stink. Especially when they're rotting in the sun. We smell battlefields long before we arrive.

All the best for your wedding, Sis. I hope this reaches you in time.

greetings from
LUNA PARK

LUNA PARK

EVENING AT 7 &
HOLIDAYS AT 2 PM

REAL PHOTO SERIES No 1777.

Dear Jim

Tom and I had a lovely few days
at St Kilda Beach. You were in our thoughts and Tom
laughed when I told him about our day at Luna Park after it opened.
Remember how we screamed on the Scenic Railway and you caught my hat
as it flew away. Who would have thought you'd sail off to war so soon afterwards?
I'd have loved a longer honeymoon, but I can't complain. With this war
dragging on, three days is more than most brides have.

Love and best wishes,

Mr and Mrs Kelly

October 1917

Dear Alice and Chook, We're on the move again. How I long to be home. I'm tending horses at a small wadi in the desert. Something is brewing. We need to be ready to march at a moment's notice.

Hello again
A quick note before we move out on another stunt. We have to evacuate the patients and pack u the tents, then set them all up again.

The Turks held a line from Gaza on the coast to Beersheba in the desert, preventing any further advance. In October 1917, the decision was made to try and take Beersheba and its strategic wells. The town was heavily defended, but an attack would not be expected from the desert.

The Light Horse set out to circle the waterless area to the east. At dawn on 31 October, artillery bombarded the Turkish trenches, then the British infantry attacked.

The Light Horse waited six miles out of town. By late afternoon time was running out. The horses hadn't drunk for two days and they could smell water. The riders gripped their reins as the Walers whinnied in frustration.

At last the signal was given. The men roared a wild coo-ee and raised their bayonets. The Walers sprang forward.

Jim rode behind with the field ambulance. He heard the horses' mad panting as he followed in their dust, then the thunder of their hooves as they approached the first trenches.

Turkish shrapnel rained overhead, but the Walers didn't falter. Even as machine-guns ripped into their lines, they galloped with all their might.

As the riders dismounted to fight, Jim moved frantically through the smoke, checking bodies, collecting those that could be saved and ferrying the wounded back to makeshift sorting stations.

$\mathcal{T}$he battle became a mad scramble of soldiers fighting hand-to-hand. Jim grabbed the reins of other riderless horses and kept his head low as he led the terrified animals back to safety.

Horsemen raced past, continuing the charge through the laneways, fighting to the far side of Beersheba.

At last the town was won. The crucial wells were in their control and the parched horses were able to drink.

When all the injured had been transferred, Jim crumpled onto the sand, exhausted. Breaker stood guard, nuzzling Jim gently until help arrived.

1 November 1917

Dear Alice

We've taken a town called Beersheba. The casualties were bad and I'm in hospital again. Don't worry, I'm not badly hurt, but when I try to stand, I shake. The doctor calls my condition shell-shock. It's a nervous condition and I've seen it in other men. The only cure is rest, but Alice, I can't rest. When I close my eyes I see impaled horses and aircraft dive-bombing our men. I was carrying one young soldier and promised to come back for another lad, but when I did, it was too late. And the horses, Alice. Their screams haunt me. Dozens were limping back without riders. Breaker copped a wound to his rump, but it's stitched and he's on the mend. I don't know what I'd do if anything happened to him. I feel such a shirker lying in bed surrounded by men with real wounds. I want to do my bit, but each time I try, I collapse.

December 1917
Another year, almost over. Still in hospital.
Your wedding photograph is on the wall beside
my bed. You were a beautiful bride, Sis. As for
Chook, what can I say? He scrubbed up well!
Congratulations on your other exciting news. I've
been daydreaming about coming home to a
nephew. Or a niece. Start looking for a pony so I
can teach the little one to ride. Surely this war
can't go on m...

February 1918
My strength is returning and I'm doing light duties. The doctor
suggested that I work away from the field for a while, so I've been
transferred again. This time to the Veterinary Corps — they're
desperately short of staff. I'm at one of the Veterinary hospitals
and I love tending the horses. The officers say I have a gift with
animals and that I should take up veterinarian studies when I
return. Imagine that! The lads organised a sing-song and a few
pints of beer for my birthday. I'm finally old enough to drink.

$\mathcal{A}$fter so much destruction, it was a relief to mend and heal animals.

As a farrier, hooves were Jim's main responsibility, but he also worked in the convalescent horse depots and hospitals. There was so much to do. Sometimes Jim followed the troops as they went out on a stoush, to give emergency care to injured horses.

Breaker enjoyed being away from the frontline. The war years had taken a toll and he was no longer young, but Breaker was reliable and Jim reckoned his horse was the steadiest mount in service.

When more horses were needed for Europe, one of the officers suggested Breaker. 'A strong trooper could be more useful over there,' he said.

But the senior veterinarian intervened. 'If Breaker goes, Jim goes. And I'm afraid Jim's become indispensable.'

15 February 1918

Dear Alice

I'm learning so much and I've been promoted again. Now I'm a Farrier Sergeant.

Last week there was an emergency with a senior veterinarian injured. I was asked to administer the anaesthetic and held a nosebag during three operations. My hands were shaking, but the doc said I did just fine.

Once this is all over, I've decided to try my hand at studying. The Veterinary Sergeant said he'd be glad to recommend me for a placement.

Another Purple Cross donation has arrived. We've received bandages, rugs and fodder bags, but best of all new surgical instruments. This will make field operations so much easier.

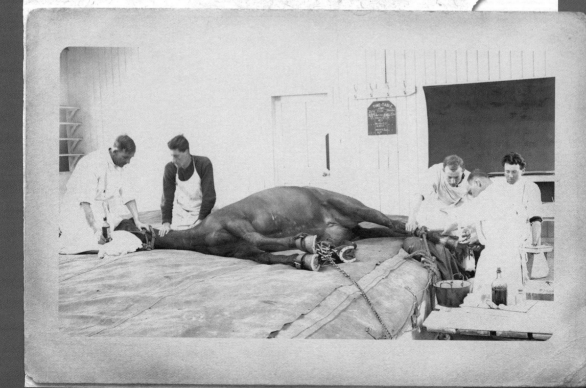

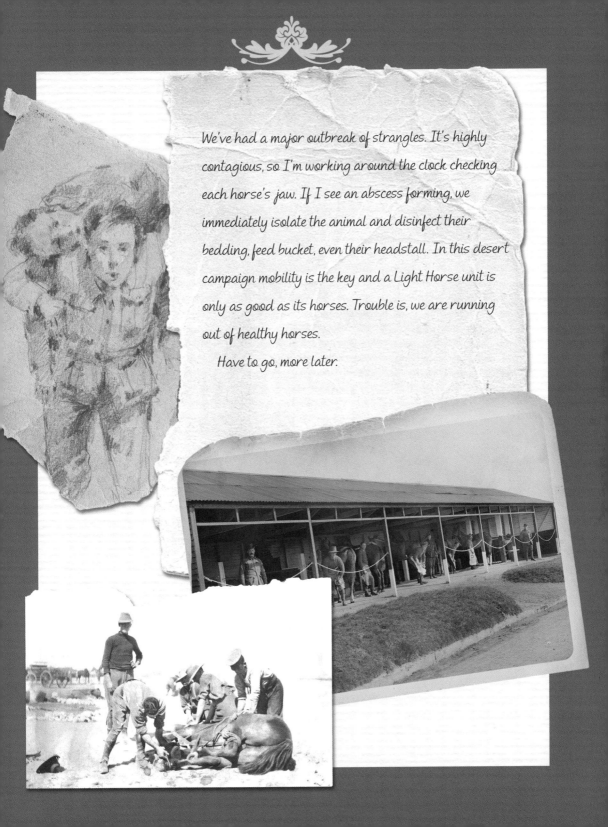

We've had a major outbreak of strangles. It's highly contagious, so I'm working around the clock checking each horse's jaw. If I see an abscess forming, we immediately isolate the animal and disinfect their bedding, feed bucket, even their headstall. In this desert campaign mobility is the key and a Light Horse unit is only as good as its horses. Trouble is, we are running out of healthy horses.

Have to go, more later.

28 February 1918

Dear Alice

Breaker and I haven't been out to check animals in the field as we've had heavy rain. It's freezing and these first two months of the year have taken a toll on the horses.

I've been busy here at the Repat Centre clipping the horses' undercarriages. After they've raised a sweat, long hair chills them. A short coat also helps reduce lice and other skin problems.

Some of the poor horses are in terri[...] very difficult for the men in the field t[...] properly, when they can hardly look [...] There never seems to be enough time [...] horses are patient for the most part [...] it seems a rum way to repay them fo[...] and loyalty.

When I'm not clipping, I've been reshoeing. We're having trouble getting remounts back into the field quickly enough. It is lucky Breaker is needed here with me, or I might lose him. The depot has been drained of all fit animals and even some of the convalescing Walers have been taken.

Further advances will be into rough country and after so many months riding through sand, the horses all need to be reshod. There aren't enough farriers so dozens of Walers are coming in with bruised feet. It breaks my heart to see shoddy shoes tearing hooves when it's so easily avoided.

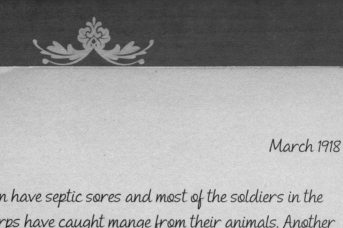

March 1918

Many men have septic sores and most of the soldiers in the Camel Corps have caught mange from their animals. Another farrier and I have packed basic veterinary supplies and we'll follow our lads as they continue the assault into the Jordan. The scenery makes a nice change, but this valley is home to snakes, scorpions and huge, black spiders that make our bandicoots look small!

*J*im received instructions to take a detour into the desert to check a suspected outbreak of glanders. The morning was fresh and Jim laughed as Breaker broke into a canter. A distant row of date palms marked the meeting place. As they approached, a figure darted behind a dune. Breaker snorted. There was a flash and suddenly the sand ahead exploded.

Jim tasted blood and everything went black. He heard a terrible horsey panting. Jim blinked, but still couldn't see. Then he felt himself falling. Jim groaned. He clutched at Breaker's mane and tried to straighten. Breaker wheezed as he struggled to raise a canter and the one thing Jim knew was that he mustn't let go.

*W*eeks later, Jim learnt that Breaker had galloped him to safety. But for now, there was only pain, blackness and drifting.

Trains whistled and clacked into Jim's shadowy world. 'Try not to move your leg,' a woman whispered. Then there were other voices: Egyptian, Indian and clipped British accents.

'Breaker,' Jim called. 'Where are you?'

There was no whinny or nickering answer.

Jim was on a stretcher. Then everything was rocking. He smelt a port. Why was it always night?

There were more soft hands.

'Alice?' he muttered.

'Sorry,' a voice replied, 'I'm not Alice. You're on a hospital ship, on your way to England. You lost a lot of blood, but you're safe. Try to rest.'

Jim reached up and felt the bandage over his eyes.

'Where's Breaker?'

There was no answer. The nurse had moved on.

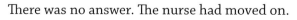

We've had a dreadful storm, Jim. The shearing shed roof peeled off and flew right into the far paddock. Lucky no one was there at the time. I thought of you and those 'khamseen'. I wonder if they're similar?

They're calling it a tornado, the strongest Melbourne storm on record. Brighton bore the brunt of it with two whirlwinds hitting at once and then a third tornado five minutes later. Two people died with many more injured.

Dearest Jim
The Horse Repatriation Centre sounds like the perfect place for you.

Tom and I were imagining you there on your birthday, surrounded by your beloved neddies. I'm so relieved that you're away from the frontline. I hope you'll be safer now.

Our Purple Cross Luncheon raised enough to buy dozens of fly veils, rugs and other equipment which we truly hope will make your lives, and those of your dear horses, more comfortable.

G'day mate
Alice has stopped feeling sick in the mornings and she's healthy (and round!). Being a dad will be a new adventure.

We still haven't heard from you. No doubt it's the mail, but Alice is worrying, so drop us a line when you can. We can't wait for this to all end so you can come home safely.

Ta Ra for now, Chook.

June 1918

Dearest Jim
Still no news from you. We're worried. Please write as soon as you can.

Dear Jim

It's been ages since we've heard from you. Tom says you're probably in the desert. Or perhaps the mail is delayed. Either way, I'm trying not to worry. Please write when you can.

All's well here. This morning we had frost on the paddocks. Last week Tom and I went across to Belgrave to have a ride on Puffing Billy. It was Tom's first time and he was leaning out the window, getting soot in his eyes — just like you did when you were nine!

Love Alice

*J*im's voyage to England was a painful blur. He drifted in and out of consciousness, searching the gloom for Charlie while Bob's children called to him and horses exploded again and again.

'Alice,' Jim moaned, trying to claw through the darkness.

He heard a chaplain whispering prayers and wondered whether he was dying.

Sometimes Jim dreamt he was riding Breaker through a pastel sunset. He swam in a murky grey canal or lazed at camp under bleached tents. Waking up to darkness after dreaming in colour was always a shock.

When Jim's hospital ship reached England, he was transferred to a hospital for the blind. Jim slumped in a chair during the day then lay in bed at night waiting for the hours to pass. Having nothing to do but think was the worst thing of all.

The one brightness was the nurses. They were kind and patient and their busy hands were soft. Especially Rose's. Jim told her about home and his fears for Breaker.

'It probably sounds silly, but I reckon I'd know if he'd been killed.'

'That's not silly,' Rose laughed. 'My mam had a touch of the knowing, as she called it. Maybe you do too.'

2 June 1918

Dear Mrs Kelly

I'm a nurse at St Dunstan's Hospital and I'm writing for your brother,
Jim, who has been transferred to us.
I am sorry to report that Jim suffered injuries to his eyes and legs.
The doctors have operated on his legs and they are mending nicely,
but at the moment Jim is unable to see. Our doctor has diagnosed
trauma blindness and it's a strange illness, Mrs Kelly. Sometimes a
patient's sight returns quickly, sometimes it takes months and sadly,
sometimes the eyesight never returns. We hope that your brother's
blindness will be temporary. In the meantime we're looking after him
as best we can.
Jim's spirits have been low, but we received a bundle of forwarded
letters from you today and that has cheered him enormously.
If you write care of the hospital, I'll make sure Jim gets your letters.

Yours Sincerely
Sister Rose

July 1918

Dear Alice and Chook

Sister Rose is writing this for me again.

My legs are stronger and now I can get about with the help of a cane. Yesterday Rose helped me hobble into the hospital garden. The smell of an English summer is a treat after all that sand. Funny how my other senses have become keener.

I still can't see, but Rose says that's not surprising, given my injuries. She has a kind voice and soft hands but now she is scolding me for saying so. The doctor will check me again next week. There's not much I can do in the meantime. The hours are long when you can't see and I feel so useless.

Hello Alice and Chook

Rose is here for my letter writing, but there's not a lot to tell. Most days I lie in the sun remembering home and my old mates.

There's a new push in ███████ They're emptying the hospital. Anyone who can help is being shipped out. Only the hopeless cases remain.

*J*im lived for the moments when Rose was able to sit by his bedside. Each time his eyes were examined, she made sure she was nearby.

'Have you seen any light at all?' the doctor asked.

'The shadows seem to change at night and sometimes I think I see flashes.'

'That's good.'

Jim clenched his hands as Rose unwrapped the bandages.

'All right, open your eyes.'

Jim blinked.

Nothing.

'Turn to me ...'

Jim turned.

The doctor's breath smelt of sausages. He held Jim's chin and peered into his eyes.

'I'm sorry, soldier,' he said at last, 'but there's no change. We'll have another look next week.'

Rose was even more gentle than usual as she rebandaged his eyes.

'What good is a blind soldier?' Jim whispered. 'I wish I'd died in battle.'

'With or without eyesight, you're a good man,' Rose said. 'A girl could do a lot worse.'

Jim turned away.

August 1918

Dear Alice

I keep wondering about Breaker. There's a rumour that when all
this ends, the Army won't be taking home the horses. After they've
given their all, it would be a rum way to repay their faithful
service. They say that horses over twelve years will be shot.
Breaker would be fourteen by now, but he always looked younger.

I ask every new soldier that arrives where he served and what he
knows about the horses. One man said there were Walers travelling
to Europe on his ship. Perhaps one of them was Breaker. I feel sure a
horse as steady as Breaker would be snapped up by an officer.

My last memory was of Breaker panting strangely as I clung
to his mane, but something inside tells me he also survived. I
guess I won't know until after the war. I'd give anything to feel
him nuzzle me again. I hate being a burden on the nurses, so I'm
learning to be more organised. Putting things in set places gives
me some independence.

This morning musicians came in to play for us. They even sang a
few Aussie tunes, so that was a treat.

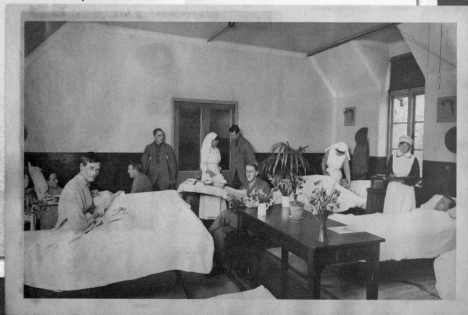

POST CARD

Dear Jim

We see more and more wounded soldiers returning and everyone says the War will soon be over. Tom and I are waiting for news of your sailing. Little Charlie is sitting up now. We show him your photograph every day.

Tom knows a saddler who would be grateful for a good leather-worker. He's a Boer War man and says he'd be proud to employ an Anzac digger.

he enemy's
offensive
failed. The
sis of the
ne between,
g German
d inflowing
levies has
gone.

have the
es in the
their vio-
nts every
objectives
they have
for the ar-
gh Ameri-
to make
defensive
have al-
he tables
exultant
ed from
ous initi-
ously af-
sition In
ess than

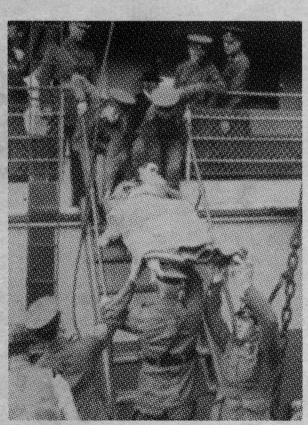

Soldiers unload our wounded heroes

Within the past month the war out look has undergone a truly marvellous change. From well-founded anxiety lest the Germans should drive home to our sore discomfiture their terrific assault on the Western battle-front, the Alli

August 1918

Dear Alice, Chook and little Charlie
I hope you're all well. I have good news.
I'll be sailing home on a merchant ship and with l[...]
before Christmas. I'll telegraph you as we get closer.

   After so many years away, I know everything will have changed. I
certainly have. More than anything I'd love to search for your
faces in the crowd as our ship pulls in, but that won't be possible.
Call my name instead so I'll know you're there.

   It will be a very different voyage without the horses to care
for. I still worry about Breaker. Will you help me write to the
Repatriation Centres after I get back? I am desperate to know what
happened to him. I've learnt to guess the hours at night and when
I'm lying here awake, I break into a sweat remembering Charlie and
Bob. I'm not the only one fighting demons. Our ward is home to
countless nightmares. In the wee hours the air is thick with
sorrow.

   But Rose has been kind enough to write my words, and this sort
of talk upsets her. Would you like to know about the weather? He[...]
   England, the days still feel warm and golden, though Rose[...]
      [f]irst leaves have turned. When we walk through the ya[...]
         [...]nder our feet.
            [...]ging to be home.
               [...]ur loving brother,

COMMONWEALTH OF AUSTRALIA.

Postmaster=General's Department, Victoria.

URGENT TELEGRAM.

This message has been received subject to the Post and Telegraph Act and Regulations.
All complaints to be addressed in writing to the Deputy Postmaster-General.

STATION FROM, No. OF WORDS, AND CHECK.

present the time lodged at at this Office respectively.

No. 45.

OFFICE DATE STAMP.

REMARKS.

BOORAL ARRIVING MELBOURNE LATE
AFTERNOON ON 28 NOVEMBER STOP

*J*im felt strangely shy as he and Rose said goodbye.

'I'll be praying that you get home safely,' she whispered.

'I reckon we'll be all right,' Jim replied. 'The Germans are too busy on the Western Front to worry about merchant shipping.'

Rose held his hand. 'Don't forget to write to me,' she said.

Before Jim could reply, he felt her lips brush his.

'Goodbye, Jim.'

Her heels hurried away and the sweet scent of tea-rose perfume was replaced by the briny smell of Liverpool's port.

A battle-weary nurse was accompanying Jim and several other patients. Her manner was brusque as she led Jim up the gangway.

'We'll need to be a bit more careful,' she scolded as his foot bumped a ledge. Jim imagined Rose giggling at this bossy matron and he suddenly wished that she was the nurse taking him home. Or that he was the one taking Rose home.

Sometimes Jim had hoped Rose was fond of him. Other times he'd thought her concern was nothing more than sympathy. What would a lass like Rose want with a broken man like him?

But she had kissed him. As Jim felt the ship roll, he wondered whether perhaps he should have told Rose how much she meant to him.

*J*im sat on the deck feeling the *Booral* roll as the swell increased. He shifted closer to the rail and thought how easy it would be to simply roll off into the sea.

'There's no shame in thinking it, mate. I reckon the shame would be acting on the thought ...'

Jim turned sharply. 'How long have you been there?' he asked.

'Not long,' the voice replied.

'Your voice sounds familiar.'

'You pulled me from the field.'

Jim searched his memories for a face. 'Curly hair ...?'

'That's me.'

'You survived.'

'They patched me up and sent me back. I copped more shrapnel in the damaged arm and they said I was permanently unfit for further active service, which doesn't do much for a chap's confidence. What about you?' Curly asked.

'Bomb blast in Palestine.'

'Will your eyes heal?'

'It's been a couple of months now and no change.'

They sat listening to the sailors go about their duties, then Curly told Jim how he'd spent the last month working at the Calais Remount Centre.

'I don't suppose you ever came across my horse?' Jim asked.

'I remember your gelding. He saved my life. You both did.' Curly paused and Jim heard a smile in his voice as he continued. 'I don't have any news about your old trooper, but there's something special I can show you.'

'What?' Jim asked.

'Take my arm ...'

Curly led him below deck and Jim breathed in the warm smell of horse and leather. Perhaps the *Booral* had been used to transport Walers.

Jim heard a whinny as Curly guided his hand towards a warm nose.

'This is Sandy,' Curly said. 'He was Major General Bridges' horse.'

The big warhorse nuzzled Jim's shoulder.

'Well, I'll be,' Curly exclaimed. 'He certainly likes you!'

Jim laughed and stroked Sandy.

'We're old mates,' he whispered as tears fell from his damaged eyes.

*J*im spent every day with Sandy and Curly. Each morning they clip-clopped around the ship's deck. Jim held Sandy's mane in one hand and his cane in the other. Following the horse matting was easy for him.

Then in the afternoons Jim helped groom Sandy. His old friend stood patiently as Jim cleaned his hooves and brushed him down. As he polished Sandy's saddle, some of Jim's confidence returned. Perhaps he could still work with horses.

The weeks passed and as they sailed closer to Western Australia, squawking seagulls swooped the deck. Jim breathed deeply and smelt the tang of eucalyptus on the breeze.

Sailors' footsteps quickened as the *Booral* neared Albany. Jim stayed out of their way on the stern, rubbing his eyes under the bandage.

He heard hooves approach, then a big warm nose nuzzled him.

'G'day,' Curly said. 'They say we'll reach King George Sound tomorrow.'

Jim slipped Sandy a lump of sugar. 'Not long to go, big fella,' he whispered. 'Soon you'll be eating your fill in a lush Melbourne paddock.'

Sandy snorted and tossed his head.

The next morning Jim rolled out of his hammock and followed a handrail to the foredeck. He recognised the stillness before dawn. Long ago smells peppered the air and Jim knew they were near land.

He braced himself against the rail, listening to the jangle of rigging. Birds called in the distance. Jim turned to where he thought east should be. He felt a flash and flinched. What was his imagination up to now?

During the past week Jim had thought he'd seen shapes, but he didn't want to be disappointed again. Not on his first day home.

He sensed another flash and Charlie's face came to mind.

Take off the bandage. What have you got to lose?

Jim reached up slowly, his fingers trembling as he untied the bandage. He blinked and Breaksea Island lighthouse flashed a welcome.

*J*im blinked again. The granite outline of an island came into focus with a lighthouse silhouetted against a magnificent pastel sky. It was the most beautiful thing Jim had seen in four terrible years. He gazed up to the heavens and whispered, 'Thank you.'

Waves crashed against the *Booral* as she sailed into King George Sound. Jim remembered the lighthouse keeper's daughter waving. He thought of his mates, lying in graves so far from home. There would be no family reunions for them at Melbourne wharf. Jim leant on the railing and wept until there were no more tears.

At last he looked up. For him, there were tomorrows. He'd survived and now he needed to live the best life he could, to honour those who wouldn't return. Jim stared ahead, remembering Rose's gentle laugh. What did she look like, he wondered? Jim imagined a sweet face to match her cheery voice. Peaches and cream skin perhaps, with bright eyes and brown hair. Or auburn hair. It didn't matter.

Jim remembered Rose saying that a girl could do worse than him. She'd also said she'd love to visit Australia. He punched the railing, realising how truly blind he'd been — but maybe it wasn't too late. He would write to Rose and tell her how he felt. If he hurried, his letter would be ready to post from Albany.

December 1919

Dear Sir

I am the Head Groom at Salisbury Downs Estate in south-west England. I write in hope of sharing some good news concerning your horse.

During the War I served at a remount centre in France. Last week I met with the fellows from my unit for an Armistice Day luncheon and one of the lads showed me the letter you sent to our War Office. We are both horse lovers and I'm not ashamed to say that your words moved me. Those horses gave their all for the cause, something some people seem to have forgotten.

Anyway, I'm writing to say that our Estate received an Australian Waler after the War. His Lordship is a fine judge of horseflesh and he was looking for a steady mount for Lady Catherine. Although old, and scarred, none of us have met a horse with a kinder temperament than this one. And he's steady. Nothing spooks him.

Lady Catherine calls him Bobby and he seems to fit your description. The gelding's original papers gave his name as Breaker. They recorded extensive war service in Palestine before he was shipped to the Calais Remount Centre. Bobby has a long white blaze and, judging by his teeth, he'd be at least fourteen years old. If this is your Breaker, please be assured that he has a home here for the rest of his days.

Lady Catherine rides him over the estate twice a week. Otherwise his time is spent grazing in a meadow with two mares and their fillies. He is also a favourite with His Lordship's grandchildren. They sneak him sugar lumps and beg to be lifted onto his broad back and led around the yard.

Well, Sir, we hope this will put an end to your search. If you are ever in England we would be honoured to receive you.

Yours sincerely in the meantime

Corporal Alistair Smith

Acknowledgements

Light Horse Boy's journey from idea to book has taken three years and during that time many people have contributed.

Firstly I would like to acknowledge the wonderful team at Fremantle Press, particularly Cate Sutherland whose wisdom has guided me over stormy seas, along the Suez and across vast deserts. Without Cate's gentle advice, occasional threats and kitbags of humour this book would not be what it is.

I am very grateful to the WA Department of Culture and the Arts. Their generous funding gave me time to write a first draft.

A huge thank you to Brian Simmonds, whose illustrations have added such depth and left me in awe of his talent — again. Thank you to photographer Helen Clark and her son, Robbie, for providing a 'face' for Brian to illustrate and thus help bring Jim to life. I am grateful to Jeff Hatwell, who kindly crosschecked details and explained the intricacies of shrapnel and battle gear. Bouquets to designer Tracey Gibbs who worked her wizardry to make the final production beautiful and authentic, and for the support of the Albany Public Library, particularly staff at the Historical Collection — Sue Smith, Julia Mitchell and Soraya Majidi.

Over the years, *Light Horse Boy* has changed shape many times. The final draft needed severe pruning to fit into 120 pages (thank you, Cate). Editing is a solitary process and I am deeply grateful to the following people for their feedback and insight when I needed fresh eyes: members of my writing group, particularly Maree Dawes, Barbara Temperton, Libby Corson and Andrew Turk. Thanks also to Venetia Marshall, Norman Jorgensen, Tracey Lawrie, Frané Lessac, Liz Newell, Kate Woodward, Karen Swallow, Audrey Davidson, Karen Davidson and David Belham.

Finally, but most importantly, I am indebted to Sophie Wolfer and Pete Watson. Your love and encouragement has kept me going when the prospect of deciphering yet another military history made me want to shred the manuscript. Thank you both.

Picture Credits

The author and publisher gratefully acknowledge the permissions granted to reproduce the copyright material in this book. Every effort has been made to trace copyright holders and to obtain permission for the use of copyright material. The author and publisher apologise for any errors or omissions and would be grateful if notified of any corrections.

Unless otherwise stated, images are from the Australian War Memorial collection: page 7, D00302; page 11, J00450; page 14, P01835.014; page 15, image courtesy Carlton Football Club; page 18, PS0092; page 19, C01624; page 21, 3073 and 2613, by kind permission of the Albany History Collection; page 24, A02440; page 25, P08286.096; page 27, H12443, EN0379 and P00117.019; page 30, P00046.049; page 31, EN0235; page 32, H01792; page 33, P00211.004 and PS0462; page 36, P01836.003; page 37, DA08445, C01521 and A04031; page 38, P09576.002; page 39, P00702.008 and newspaper copy from *Sydney Mail*, 26 May 1915, page 7; page 42, J05589; page 43, P05290.001 and A02867; page 46, G00269 and H16647; page 52, C00662; page 53, PS1514; page 56, P01815.005; page 57, J04734 and H03061; page 61, H02732 and C00386; page 64, H11710 and P02132.001; page 65, P00153.014 and B00168; page 68, H00678; page 69, P01815.019 and H12548V; page 70, B02465; page 71, B02667; page 74, J01081; page 75, H00725; page 76, H91.93/53 courtesy of State Library of Victoria and 1915, by kind permission of the Albany History Collection; page 77, P00143.001 and J06564; page 82, J05572; page 83, P00562.181; page 86, E04440; page 87, E04427 and H02674; page 88, B01565; page 89, B00007; page 95, Puffing Billy Archives, courtesy John Thompson; page 98, H18889; page 99, P03787.003; page 102, D00569; page 103, H11573 and newspaper copy from *The Argus*, 17 August 1918, page 16; page 105, H11576.

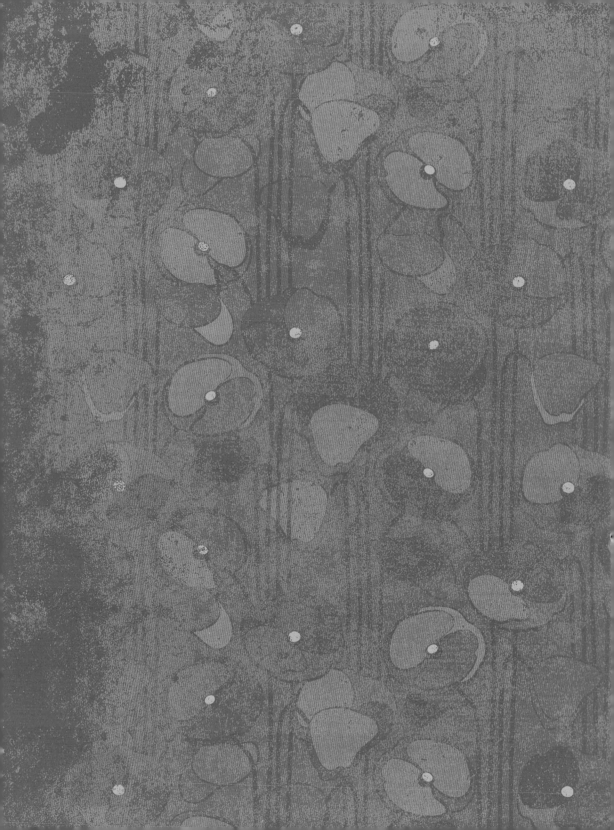